D0004175

Text © 2002 by Mahlon F. Craft
Illustrations © 2002 by Kinuko Y. Craft
All rights reserved.

The artwork for this book was prepared by using oil over
watercolor on Strathmore™ illustration board.
The text for this book is set in Adobe Koch Antiqua.
Book design by Mahlon F. Craft.
Manufactured in China.

Library of Congress Cataloging-in-Publication Data
is available.

A CIP catalogue record for this book is available from
The British Library.

ISBN 1-58717-120-1 (trade edition)
ISBN 1-58717-121-X (library edition)

Distributed in Canada by Raincoast Books
9050 Shaughnessy Street, Vancouver, British Columbia
V6P 6E5

10 9 8 7 6 5 4 3 2

Chronicle Books LLC
85 Second Street, San Francisco, California 94105

www.chroniclekids.com

For hope

nce upon a time there lived a King and Queen whose fondest desire was to have a child — "A little one to bounce on our knee," as they wistfully said every day. A year passed, then three, yet they remained without child still.

Just when the loving couple thought their wish would remain forever unfulfilled, the Queen began to bathe at a secluded pool where there lived an ancient frog. She sang to the old creature as sweetly as she would to a child of her own. To the Queen's great surprise, one day the frog sprang from his perch and began to speak. "To one far more fair than I should song so sweet be sung. Within twelve months' time a daughter to you shall be born."

And just as the frog said, a little girl was soon born to the Queen. The King was so overcome with joy that he could barely contain himself. The child was called Aurora, and the King ordered a great christening feast to celebrate. Every relative, friend, and any other acquaintance of importance was invited, and the royal squires were sent to search out all of the fairies who inhabited his realm.

ow it happened that to invite the fairies required very special golden place settings for each. The King had just twelve and they were very costly indeed — even for a king. When the squires returned and announced that thirteen fairies were living in his lands, the King became quite vexed, for his treasuries were nearly as dear to him as his daughter. But when he learned the thirteenth was a very old fairy who had not been seen for more than fifty years, the King happily concluded, "She must be either dead or under some spell. Surely there is no need to inquire further."

When at last the ceremonies were over, the guests retired to the King's palace where the attendance of the fairies was to be celebrated at the feast. Each of the twelve places was set in magnificent style indeed, with plates and cups of beaten gold and a jewelled chest containing a knife, fork, and spoon, all inlaid with precious stones. The table was laid with bowls and glasses of crystal and all was set aglitter by candles too numerous to count.

After a splendid meal each fairy presented the child with a magic gift. One gave virtue, another wisdom, a third beauty, and so on, until the Princess Aurora had been assured nearly every good fortune in life. Just as the eleventh fairy bestowed her wish, the thirteenth fairy — who was very much alive after all — appeared in a flash.

nd now you may have MY gift!" the old fairy exclaimed angrily. "On her sixteenth birthday, the Princess shall prick herself with a spindle and die!" Without another word, she turned and stormed out of the hall.

The fearful prophecy caused the guests to shudder, and the gentler souls among them wept. Almost out of their wits with grief, the King and Queen now despaired of the terrible cost of the King's rash and selfish decision to ignore the thirteenth fairy.

But now the twelfth fairy, whose gift was still unspoken, stepped forward. "Your Majesties! Calm yourselves. Although my powers cannot alter my elder sister's terrible wish, the Princess shall not die. Instead Aurora shall fall into a deep sleep that will last one hundred years."

With that, she and all of the rest of the fairies vanished.